ELF HELP

http://www.falala.com

MARGIE PALATINI

ILLUSTRATED BY MIKE REED

HYPERION BOOKS FOR CHILDREN · NEW YORK

First Edition

1 3 5 7 9 10 8 6 4 2

The artwork for each picture is prepared using acrylic paints.
This book is set in 18-point Pike.

Library of Congress Cataloging-in-Publication Data
Palatini, Margie.
Elf Help : http://www.falala.com / Margie Palatini ; illustrated by Mike Reed.—1st ed.
p.   cm.
Summary: When Alfred E. Elf decides to use a computer to prepare the list of good boys and girls for Santa, he causes quite a
mix-up.
ISBN 0-7868-0359-2 (trade)—ISBN 0-7868-2304-6 (lib. bdg.)
[1. Elves—Fiction. 2. Santa Claus—Fiction.] I. Reed, Mike, 1951-   ill.
II. Title.
PZ7.P1755El   1998
[E]—dc21   96-53314

ELF HELP

http://www.falala.com

Alfred was not an ordinary, everyday,
jinglebell-jingling, workshop-working elf.
He flunked Wrapping 101. Big time.
Curl a ribbon?
Tie a bow?
Don't think so.
Stuff a stocking? This elf? Forget about it.
And Alfred didn't have a clue
how to build, paint, or even glue
one single, solitary, Santa-lovin' toy.

B
ut, while Arnold Elf was Santa's number one toy stacker . . .

And Andrew Elf was Santa's number one toy packer . . .

It was Alfred E. who was the one and only, wiz-of-a-wonk computer hacker. At least he wanted to be. (Actually, Alfred worked in the mail room.)

But he was an elf with some Christmas dreams of his own. And plans. Big plans.

S o on the night before Christmas,
when all through Santa's house
every other elf was hurrying and scurrying,
Alfred was busy clicking on his mouse.

Clickety-click click. Clickety-click click.
"Alfred!"
Clickety-click click. Clickety-click click.
"Alfred!"
Clickety-click click. Clickety-click click.
"AL-FRED!"

Olcott J. Elf, Chief Elf of Operations, was not very merry.
He folded his arms and tapped a curled toe.
"Elf! You're late!" said the CEO.
"Where's Santa's list of toys for all the good
little girls and boys? The Big Guy is
dashing off in five minutes.
Jingle those bells and
mistletoe it on up to
the roof. Move it!"

Alfred gulped. His toes tingled. This was his big chance.
But could he, would he, should he?
No ordinary, old-fashioned Christmas List for Santa this year.
No sirree. He'd show 'em.

Alfred opened his Frosty Windows
and searched for his special super-duper Elf File.

He scanned.

Scrolled.

Rolled.

And with a quick double click
he did a download on his elf code, and he was—
"Alfred E. Elf, reporting front and center, Santa, sir.
Pre~senting the Saint Nick-Net, Mega-Merry, CyberSanta
Christmas List! Completely holiday high-tech."

Santa nosed up his specs
and stared at the shiny silver disk.

"OH? OH! O-O-OH."

"It's totally yule-proof, sir," said Alfred.
"Elf guaranteed. I made the list. Checked it twice.
Found out who was naughty. Found out who was nice."
Santa scratched his chin and rubbed his belly.
Did he really hear what he had heard?
Santa on-line! Olcott J. raised an eyebrow.
"This is totally absurd! Elf! Did you see when they were
sleeping? Do you know when they're awake?"

Alfred nodded. "And I know if they've been bad or good.
My Elfcheck is good, for goodness' sake! I logged in each and
every wish from each and every tot. Skates. Dolls. Books. Blocks.
Yup. I gave my it best one-two crunch."

Olcott rolled his eyes and mumbled, "Holy holly.
This elf is out to lunch!"

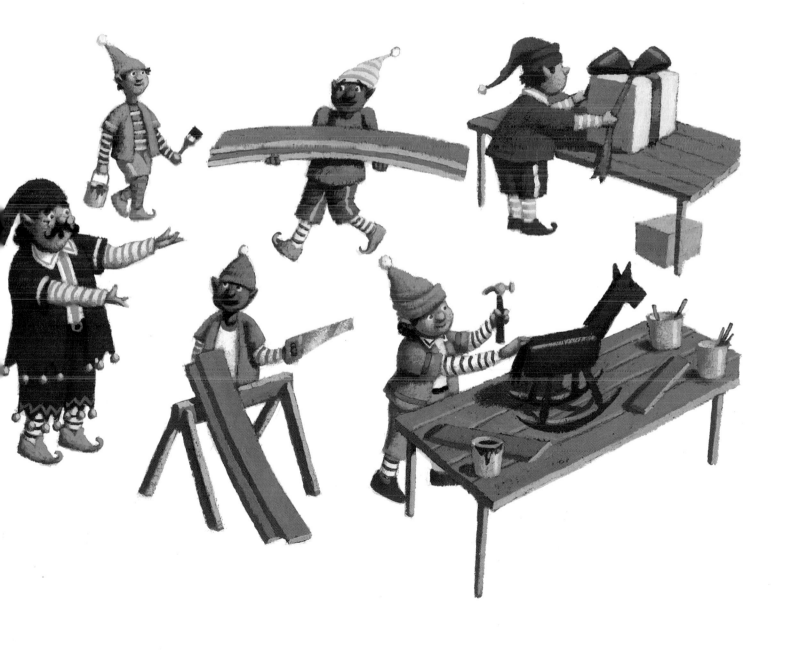

"Face the fax, Chief," said Alfred. "It's the new millennium!
Time for Santa to surf the net.

"Weave a web.

"Dish the disk.

"I've got the old sleigh totally wired with RAM, ROM,
and more bit and byte than Vixen and Blitzen
can nibble, munch, or chew. *CyberSanta.*
Trust me, Mr. C. It's you. It's you. It's you!"

"Whoa, Whoa, Whoa!" Santa looked downright dizzy.

"Yes, Alfred, hold your horses and rein in Rudolph.
CyberSanta, indeed!" Olcott shook his head and whispered
as Santa leaned an ear his way. "Sorry, sir. A 'Valley Elf.'
I'm afraid he's just not North Pole material."

"Oh, no no!" Santa said with a twinkle.

"The sprite's got spirit. I'm on-line with you, Alfred."

With a wink to the wonk and a pat on the head.

Alfred knew right there and then, he had nothing to dread.

With a wave and a jingle, to his team Santa gave the call.

Then they dashed away—dashed away—dashed away all.

A

lfred went back to the mail room happy.

Quite content, very proud.

He kicked off his shoes and unpointed his cap.

He leaned back.

Stretched.

Yawned.

Hey! He deserved it! He took a bit of a nap.

Alfred snored and snoozed. Snoozed and snored.

Why, he was so tired he slept right through Christmas Eve
and well past Christmas morning.

But not the children. Oh, no. Not the children.

Little Johnny Chester at 923 East 83rd Street, New York, N. Y.,
woke up bright and early Christmas morning
and ran to the tree in apartment 3D to look for ice skates.

But little Johnny Chester didn't see skates
under that tree in apartment 3D. *Naaaaaaa-aaaaayyy!*

Little Johnny Chester saw a horse!

A horse?

A *horse!*

While way out west in Tucson, Arizona,
at the Yippee-Aye-A Ranch—*Aye Yi Yi!*
No horse of course for little Connie Lester.
It was Connie, not Johnny,
who found ice skates.
But where was the ice?
This was not very nice.

Jenny Parker, from sunny California,
looked under her tree for a surfboard.
But Jenny Parker didn't find a board to surf.
It was up in Nome, Alaska,
on Kenny Barker's snowy turf.

Jenny Parker got skis. Skis?
Oh, Jeez Louise!

It was Mary Louise Miller who
got long woolly socks,

while Gary Louis Diller
got a bunch of cuckoo clocks.

And poor Mikey Stiller got somebody's—
who knows whose—rocks! Rocks?
Piled high in a box!

Moms and Dads were not amused. Not amused at all.
It didn't take long before Alfred's fax machine was humming—
and messages were coming—fast and furious.
And his E-mail was stuffed full
with parents' not-so-cheery chatter.
Alfred jumped to his feet when he heard all the clatter.

He ran to his computer to see what was the matter.

He clicked on his Frosty Windows.

The Alfred Elf Line burped,

beeped,

then flashed!

Oh no! This was terrible! His computer had just crashed!

"**W**hat's going on here?" shouted Olcott J. Elf.

"Oh, uh . . . just a bit of a meltdown, Chief.

There seems to be a little glitch."

"A little glitch? Try a humongous switch!

You and that computer have ruined Christmas!

Explain yourself, Elf!"

But Alfred had no answer.

Had he hit the wrong buttons? Crossed the wrong keys?

Fa-la-la'd when he should have ho-ho-ho'd?

"Just get it unmixed and fixed," growled the Chief.

"And now! Or this will be the last Christmas

you hear another ho, ho, ho."

"Ooooh-oooh-oooh," moaned Alfred.

His goose was cooked.

He had clicked his last click, bit his last byte.

It looked like there was nothing for him to do

but pack up and head south.

And then, just as Alfred stuffed his last striped stocking into his sack and Olcott J. was showing him the door, a little white note floated down from Santa's old mail chute.

"Look, Chief!" cried Alfred, reading the letter. "Look! Look! Christmas wasn't ruined after all!"

"*One* letter, Alfred?" said Olcott, very unimpressed. "One puny little note and you think that closes the book on this boo-boo? No way!"

Dear Santa,

How did you know I always wanted a horse? Mr. Ned is already my best friend. This was the best gift I never asked for.

Love,
Johnny Chester

Alfred stood under the mail chute and looked up. "Way!"

"I beg your pardon, Elf?" shouted Olcott.

"Oh! OH! I mean—away, Chief! Move out of the way. Way, way, way out of the way!" Alfred cried, running for cover.

First came two letters. Then four.

And more.

And more!

And more!

Suddenly there was an avalanche of letters

and notes, postcards and papers—

a merry megadrop of mail, all thanking Santa

for the best Christmas presents ever!

Dear Santa,

Mom and Dad said,
rocks in a box? I of course
knew they were way cool
blocks! They really rock!
Thanks, Santa.
This is the best
present of my whole life!

Love,
Mikey

Dear Santa,

Why ski when you
can surf! A "snow" board!
Totally cool, Santa.

Your friend,
Kenny

To S
Nor

The kids didn't think it was a mix-up at all!

They liked it! They liked it! . . . Even Mikey!

Dear Santa,
You made ice! You're
so nice! This is the
first time in 102 years
that we had snow for
Christmas. And thanks
to you, I had ice
skates! Yippee-Aye-A!

Love,
Connie Lester

Dear Santa,
How did you guess?
I'm cuckoo for cuckoo
clocks!

Thank you.
Thank you.
Thank you.

Gary Louis Diller

"Jingle my bells and uncurl my toes. The kids are happy!
Well, what do you know," said the CEO, climbing out from
under a heap of thank-yous. "Don't ask me how,
but it looks like you did it after all, you little hacker!"

"I did?" Alfred was more than a bit
and a byte surprised himself.

Olcott read letter after letter and then gave Alfred
a pat on the back.

Dear
Santa,

"I think there just might be
a little Christmas bonus
in your stocking this year,
Elf. You're movin' on up."

Well, Alfred was so happy
he positively beamed.
Who would have thunk it?
He got the Christmas wish he'd dreamed!
Alfred sighed a mega-cybersigh.
Whew! Christmas was still
Christmas after all.

And although he couldn't
explain it, try as hard as he might . . .

Even with an elf on the computer,

somehow everything still turned out all right.